AF081305

Three Loves

30 Sonnets on Love for God, Others, and Self

Rhodesia

Ukiyoto Publishing

All global publishing rights are held by

Ukiyoto Publishing

Published in 2023

Content Copyright © Rhodesia

ISBN 9789360162610

*All rights reserved.
No part of this publication may be reproduced, transmitted, or stored in a retrieval system, in any form by any means, electronic, mechanical, photocopying, recording or otherwise, without the prior permission of the publisher.*

The moral rights of the authors have been asserted.

This is a work of fiction. Names, characters, businesses, places, events, locales, and incidents are either the products of the author's imagination or used in a fictitious manner. Any resemblance to actual persons, living or dead, or actual events is purely coincidental.

This book is sold subject to the condition that it shall not by way of trade or otherwise, be lent, resold, hired out or otherwise circulated, without the publisher's prior consent, in any form of binding or cover other than that in which it is published.

www.ukiyoto.com

Dedication

This anthology is heartily dedicated to all who believe in the power and glory of love, as exemplified in the love of and for God, others and oneself.

To the Almighty.

To my loved ones, late father Rudy, mother Evelyn, and children Liana and Rodemil.

To all my friends, present and future, who are as countless as the stars.

To Ukiyoto Publishing, my sincerest thanks for providing a pathway for this book to be shared to the world.

Contents

Introduction	1
Love For God	3
I Love You, Lord	4
I Seek You	5
I Trust in Him	6
Divine Guidance	7
My Father	8
I Will Declare	9
The Wonder of Your Love	10
What is Faith?	11
Ask and Reap	12
Redemption	13
Love for Others	14
True Tale	15
My Only Love	16
Tests of Fire	17
Mirage	18
The Spark	19
Home	20
Miracles	21

Sufficient	22
One Happy Family	23
Best Friend	24
Love for Self	25
I Set Me Free	26
All Due Respect	27
Mirror	28
Fortify	29
Chill	30
Inner Peace	31
Fountain of Joy	32
Be Well	33
I'm Perfectly Imperfect	34
Jubilation	35
About the Author	*36*

Introduction

"The only magic man will ever need,
To connect chasms is for love to lead."

This gift called *love* is one of the greatest blessings bestowed to man. For those who have experienced its zenith, they may relate to the bliss and elation vis-à-vis the pain needed to be endured for love to withstand the test of time. This bittersweet experience traverses the full spectrum of love from the love of God to man who disobeys Him, the love of Christ who got injured, insulted and died to atone for man's transgressions, the patient and enduring love of a mother to her son, and the faithful love of two souls torn apart by unfavorable circumstances. Love has many forms and seasons, but has to endure many tests and tribulations to emerge true, no less than gold to acid, or diamond to heat and pressure.

This book is an anthology of Shakespearean sonnets, which are rhythmic, rhyming poems of fourteen lines and ten syllables per line, with the pattern *ababcdcdefefgg*. More than the form, this book is a celebration of different facets of love, divided into three sections - Love for God, Love for Others, and Love for Self. The Love for Others include mostly romantic love, love for children, love for friends, love for neighbors, and love for humanity. A separate section is dedicated to the love for self, which is very crucial but neglected by many. Even the scriptures teach us to love others as ourselves, for we cannot pour from an empty cup. If we can enrich our hearts and lives, we can share more to the world in terms of love, value and resources; but first, we should take care of ourselves.

Like the previous written works of Rhodesia, which include *"Words of Wisdom," "Houses," and "A New Beginning,"* this book aims to perpetuate love, faith, and hope to humanity, and raise the prevailing vibration of the collective to genuine and infinite love.

Love For God

I Love You, Lord

(Love is humbling.)

I love You Lord, though I am but a speck,
Afloat in an expanse of multiverse
Of stars, planets, black holes, and fiery flecks,
No human being ever lived traversed.
I love You Lord, though my life is fleeting,
A silent segment of eternity,
A fading rainbow, a meteor passing,
A transient moment of infinity.
I love You Lord, though I am just a piece
Among your multitude of creations,
A single soul in throngs of entities,
A thread of life in the thick of zillions.
Despite my minuteness, I pledge You love,
All of me and all I can ever have.

I Seek You

(Love seeks, and finds.)

I seek Your frame, my Lord, in every way,
Your eyes peer from the stars in thick of night,
Your warm embrace that wakes us up each day,
Embodied in the sun that smiles so bright.
Your breath I smell in morning mountain breeze,
The birds echo your voice in dawn chorus,
Your delighted eyebrows in rainbows freeze,
Your touch as soft as petals of the rose.
I hear You laugh in a baby's giggle,
As if to herald hope and victory,
I see you wince in man's daily struggle,
Your semblance most defined in mystery.
In awe and wonder of the universe,
Alas, I spot an outline of Your face.

I Trust in Him

(Love trusts.)

I passed through shady alleys in a slum,
And climbed a towering hill all alone,
In the midst of turbulence, I am calm,
Because the Lord is my stronghold and home.
The enemies may weave a thousand lies,
And place a snare to humiliate my name,
They may arrange all coaxing to entice,
But God will lift me out from all their blame.
I've no vast wealth or power in this world,
No mansion, costly car, or luxury,
My comfort is communion with my Lord,
Whose eternal grace frees me from worry.
I'm peaceful and content, I plan, I dream,
I have no fear because I trust in Him.

Divine Guidance

(Love follows.)

In a world voracious for liberty,
For unrestricted freedom of movement,
Questioning limits, pushing boundaries,
The Lord laid down safeguards and commandments.
Not to restrain, or chain, or imprison,
But to ensure the humans He cares for,
Will not shatter in reckless abandon,
Instead blossom and flourish all the more.
The precepts of God are food for the soul,
His teachings radiant light to guide our path,
To establish our lives for the long haul,
And save us from the misery of wrath.
Still, He gave us the power to decide,
Whether or not in His guidance abide.

Three Loves

My Father

(Love guides.)

You are my Father God who held my hand,
When I was a baby full of giggles,
In your steady guidance, I learned to stand,
You supported me in all my struggles.
You are my Father God who held me tight,
When I was scared to trudge far from our home,
You helped me learn, you brought me to the light,
In knowledge and experience I was honed.
You are my Father God who led my path,
As I was scouting for a vocation,
Sometimes through a storm and its aftermath,
You helped me discover my life mission.
You are my Father God, and I am safe,
In you I trust my life, with solid faith.

I Will Declare

(Love declares.)

I will declare the marvel of Your love,
How You have blessed my life from day to day,
I neither was astray nor did I starve,
You rescued me from dangers on my way.
I will impart Your glory to my clan,
So they may also bask in Your wonder,
We'll praise Your name, and heed Your divine plan,
To dwell with You in heaven forever.
I will proclaim Your tender salvation,
To strangers, comrades, and acquaintances,
All of us direly need Your compassion,
For our transgressions, be graced forgiveness.
My Lord, I'll sing and cheer your Holy name,
To share the light of Your eternal flame.

The Wonder of Your Love

(Love adores.)

The universe suspends in Your great force,
Each object in the right coordinate,
So planets may revolve in proper course,
Bearing the life You made to perpetuate.
The cell you fashioned in the best design,
Like a miniscule country of its own,
With borders, set of laws, and troops assigned,
And smartest powerhouses ever known.
This Earth You gave to be man's cozy home,
Still teems with beauty in its innate state,
Where plants You set to sustain life have grown,
Your love permeates in every breath we take.
My Lord, the wonder of your love is great,
In You, we fully rest our steadfast faith.

What is Faith?

(Love believes.)

The earth harbors a plethora of life,
Otters build houses, and elephants mourn,
All living things breed and adopt to strife,
Have special faculties since they were born.
What makes mankind the most special being,
Unique and prevailing over the world,
Is not even language, wit, or feeling,
But the right for communion with the Lord.
Whatever culture, religion, or clan,
It's as if faith in the genes is programmed,
Innate is our hope for a higher plan,
The need to worship is deeply ingrained.
What then is faith, but nature and essence?
A greater appendage, a higher sense.

Ask and Reap

(Love connects.)

Before we rise from bed each brand new day,
Let's pause, and set intentions to be met,
Then to the Lord Almighty ask and pray,
He listens to and blesses goals we set.
Along the road, we may encounter blocks,
At times too big for us, we think it's end,
But help does come to one who surely asks
The Lord who knows the way around the bend.
Our strength may fail before the task is through,
No matter how we squeeze, our force is void,
There is a Source who can restore us new,
When we succeed, He too is overjoyed.
As humans we have our limitations,
Apt to ask and reap Divine connection.

Redemption

(Love forgives.)

Our God, You have the best aspirations,
For the man you cherish and treasure most,
Your dearest child, Your most prized creation,
Chose not to heed Your guidance and was lost.
Until today, we still fall slave to sin,
Though You have laid Your counsel to instruct,
We let the weakness in our nature win,
In Your despair, we willed to self-destruct.
Indeed, you can allow us to be damned,
Yet Your love's broader than the universe,
To rescue us from sin, You sent Your son,
Who suffered for our lot to be reversed.
Our lives are bright and hopeful as You bless
Our redemption, mercy, and forgiveness.

Love for Others

True Tale

(Love bridges.)

Once upon a time, in an old kingdom,
There lived a handsome and successful prince,
Beknown for his boundless wealth and wisdom,
That no one had experienced ever since.
Far from the castle lived a simple maid,
Contented with what little things she had,
In spite of all the trials she had stayed
A buoyant vibrant girl immune to sad.
In playful toss of fate these two souls met,
The plain girl filled his highness' emptiness,
In purity and innocence she set
His heart in true and lasting happiness.
The only magic man will ever need,
To connect chasms is for love to lead.

Three Loves

My Only Love

(Love is faithful.)

It's been eons since I last saw your face,
But your image is still etched in my heart,
No matter how far we moved on our ways,
The love we share will never ever part.
It doesn't matter where on earth you are,
Inside my mind is where you'll always live,
Our story has been written on the stars,
And will come true as long as we believe.
In our journey away from each other,
Someone else may want to patch our longing,
Perhaps more charming, mature, or kinder,
But not the lost half our soul is yearning.
Whatever complication we may have,
You will forever be my only love.

Tests of Fire

(Love endures.)

In most dire circumstance a love was born,
With it, a grain of faith and glimpse of hope,
That brought forth gush of joy in every morn,
And perfect peace, for all contentions cope.
Despite vast distance and harsh obstacles,
These two hearts beat for each other alone,
When even just to meet claimed miracles,
They remained each other's refuge and home.
At times, their stances risked to separate
What even time and distance could not part,
But not too long; there was no space for hate,
Where hearts are filled with overflowing love.
All tests of fire they're able to withstand,
For every day, they faced life hand in hand.

Mirage

(Love hopes.)

I dream a future with the one I love,
Together in a place so sweet and calm,
Through ups and downs, inseparable halves,
In summer or storm, walking hand in hand.
I see him dry the teardrops from my eyes,
I hear him laugh that fills my heart with songs,
I feel the warmth of his tender embrace,
Only with him, my heart and soul belongs.
We'll have a home that's filled with love and joy,
A cozy place where our young ones roam free,
And life need not be rushed but just enjoyed,
Making and leaving happy memories.
My love and I will share eternal rest,
And never part in our heavenly nest.

The Spark

(Love inspires.)

You are the spark that lit my lofty thoughts,
The current that electrifies my pen,
You are the archetype I've always sought,
To be my victor versus all villains.
You are the sun that wakes me up at morn,
A breathtaking day to look forward to,
You are my every wish, my hope reborn,
The world's a dazzling place because of you.
In every typhoon, you are my rainbow,
The darkest clouds lined by your silver smile,
I look forward to every tomorrow,
Your hand in mine, we'll walk a thousand miles.
You're my only beau, my inspiration,
My strength and vigor, my sole devotion.

Home

(Love secures.)

Sometimes a place, oftentimes a person,
A secret sacred space, a sanctuary,
Where not only offsprings, but dreams are born,
A shelter of lasting peace and safety.
When faced with sadness and desolation,
Or threatened with a devastating storm,
During uncertainties and confusion,
We retreat to the comfort of our home.
Within its warm embrace we're kept from cold,
Within its stable arms we're safe and fed,
Its hands are firm with vow to have and hold,
The heart that senses and fulfills our needs.
A home is where we feel the most secure,
Because limitless genuine love is poured.

Miracles

(Love takes care.)

Every second we witness miracles
Unfolding right before our very eyes,
If we but tend to note the spectacle
Of bringing forth to earth another life.
What great honor to be an instrument
In kindling such unique and special souls,
In taking part in their development,
In watching them emerge from wee to full.
Along with them the heavens gift us love,
The torrent of emotions bring forth care,
To nurture and to mold, to heed and have,
To never mind the sacrifices spared.
Behold the joy of giving up our own,
Just to secure they'll thrive who we have sown.

Sufficient

(Love shares.)

The island breeze almost blew off their lamp,
Their only light each night in their small home,
Eight mouths to dine and share the meager lump,
While praying for their safety from the storm.
Not from afar a mansion on a hill,
Glittering like heaven flooded with stars,
With only four to feed, their graces spill,
To servants and beloved animals.
Perhaps there's no food insufficiency,
For the growing human population,
If we can only see where our plenty,
Can rescue another's destitution.
There is no lack if we can only care,
For our excesses to the needy share.

One Happy Family

(Love unites.)

We may be multitude in various lands,
With different tongues, features, and culture,
But deep within our hearts we understand,
In diversity, we craft our future.
We share a common earth and universe,
That speck in space we fondly call our home,
The common air we breathe just circulates,
One sun, one moon, linked waters, and one dome.
The thoughts and emotions of each of us,
Are waves in the sea of humanity,
Love, joy, faith, or hope, despair or trespass,
Move mankind in shared synchronicity.
We are, after all, one big family,
Let each dwell peacefully and happily.

Best Friend

(Love lasts.)

When we were young, we held each other's hands,
And listened to one another's stories,
'Twas nice to have someone who understands,
And cares about our private reveries.
When the world seemed to turned its back on me,
You stayed, and never let me be alone,
When you were sick, I was your family,
Your unfailing and constant companion.
When you were wed, I was maid of honor,
And you, the closest kin of my children,
Our lives had bloomed from simple to splendor,
From smooth to wrinkled, from teen to golden.
So much time erodes, still we kept in touch,
You're my best friend, I love you very much.

Love for Self

I Set Me Free

(Love frees.)

I love myself enough to set me free,
From whatever bondage I got entwined,
No other hero will come rescue me,
As long as slavery ties up my mind.
I am not a servant of circumstance,
If ever I may be deprived or grieved,
I will convert misfortune to a chance
For what may seem impossible achieved.
I am not bound to place or even time,
I'll travel like a tourist due for treat,
I give myself the right to wish sublime,
And realize the urge of my spirit.
I reclaim, own, and control my power,
To no oppressor ever surrender.

All Due Respect

(Love respects.)

What would a world feel like when all respect
The rights and views of others and one's own?
In all things, there may be various facets,
The entirety of truth cannot be known.
We all may voice our mind and opinion,
While listening to others' points of view,
For all we know, there may be a union,
A greater us, a better me and you.
Yet first, we learn to love and value self,
To hear the promptings of our heart and soul,
Our emotions need not be put to shelf,
But celebrated as a gift to all.
When each of us is valued and esteemed,
The richness of diversity will teem.

Mirror

(Love accepts.)

When you face a mirror, what do you see?
Too pale, or too dark skin, too curly hair?
Or can you stare at your unique beauty,
That only you and none other can share?
When you look at yourself, how do you feel?
Do you loathe or abhor the way you're shaped?
Or can you accept all of you that's real,
And gift yourself the love you well deserve?
Everytime you see your own reflection,
Push your chin up, smile, and open your chest,
Spoil yourself with your own adoration,
You're beautiful, and worth living your best.
No one else journeys life with you, but you,
Might as well believe in your own self too.

Fortify

(Love enhances.)

How else to love oneself but educate,
Each day, furnish the mind with new knowledge,
Do not let capability stagnate,
To hone one's skill sets is to acknowledge.
Read, observe, learn, practice, and experience,
The world offers infinite stratagem,
To sharpen and expand intelligence,
From which our outputs and creations stem.
The growth of information is so swift,
So is the progress of technology,
We need equip ourselves to stay and drift,
With updated new age literacy.
To constantly adopt, our battle cry,
With knowledge, skills, and wisdom fortify.

Chill

(Love calms.)

Cool down, sit back, relax and learn to chill,
When work is accomplished, or the day done,
At times, we get more productive when still,
And tasks done easier while having fun.
Even the brain, to function at its peak,
To clear its webs, make sense of day's events,
Needs to slow down and get a good night's sleep,
While it uploads to memory times spent.
For a moment, free yourself from pressure,
Feel your heartbeat, and listen to your breath,
Look at the skies, experience the pleasure,
Of being just alive, blessed with good health.
Close your eyes, go within, and celebrate,
The time is yours to rest and recreate.

Inner Peace

(Love soothes.)

To sleep like a baby throughout the night,
With no chiding whispers from the conscience,
The body is tired, but the heart is light,
Remembering the day's sweet experience.
To wake up fully rested and recharged,
As the smiling sun warmly greets good morn,
New chances await in a world so large,
There is hope and faith in a love reborn.
Minor offenses are not worth the time,
Or the energy better directed
To fulfilling the heart's wishes sublime,
Than to petty, kiddy quarrels scattered.
To focus on the good, and slights dismiss,
Will grant each day a priceless inner peace.

Fountain of Joy

(Love enjoys.)

Do we need a reason to feel content?
Should we require our hearts to fill with things,
With objects from without, for merriment?
Or are all feelings just imaginings?
Some people scout the world for happiness,
In thrill and pleasure, wealth and adventure,
A few clearly accept they're truly blessed,
Enjoying each day, life's simple treasures.
That joy and bliss elusive to many,
Sits still inside our hearts should we just heed,
To smile, to laugh, to purely be happy,
Feel it, and we will be radiant indeed.
The manner of glee will open our eyes,
The fountain of joy is naught but inside.

Be Well

(Love pampers.)

The water's so refreshing to be timed,
Soak and relax leisurely in the tub,
Smile, your life will turn out as you designed,
Just be yourself, and live the life you love.
On special events, be the first to greet
Your very own self on a festive day,
Be the one who gives yourself the best gift,
You merit to be served the finest way.
Choose tastefully the clothes you slip into,
Dress how you want yourself to feel within,
And not how anyone else want you to,
Because you're not their doll to just fit in.
Feel good, and be your person who pampers,
Be well, soon more flow from the universe.

I'm Perfectly Imperfect

(Love jives.)

I may not have the physique to grace covers,
Or skin as smooth and dewy as a glass,
In my lifetime, I've had epic blunders,
For some, I've been repeatedly harassed.
Yes, I may not be a perfect package,
And all you see is just the genuine me,
I need no fancy mask, or full baggage,
I am enough to serve society.
My crevices and flaws fit other's strengths,
The weakness of each one binds us the most,
Thus, I too have my own unique talents,
To contribute and fill what others lost.
I'm perfectly imperfect and belong,
To Earth, our perfectly imperfect home.

Jubilation

(Love celebrates.)

There's always a reason to celebrate,
Everytime the heart beats and mind thinks clear,
Ourselves at times we need congratulate,
Like in dire situations, how well we steer.
For every hurdle passed, or illness healed,
For reunited love, and newborn babe,
For questions answered, mysteries revealed,
For pain endured, until a gain is made.
Success is not for others to define,
When each person has his own unique goal,
With individual plan, trail, and design,
Unmatched like fingerprints in every soul.
Rejoice and cherish realizations,
We all merit cheer and jubilation.

About the Author

Rhodesia

Rhodesia is a physician, poet, painter, author and devoted mother of two brilliant kids.

Among her published works are, "Words of Wisdom," "Houses," and "A New Beginning," which are inspirational prose and poetry intended to uplift the vibration of humanity to that of sublime love, peace, and joy.

www.ingramcontent.com/pod-product-compliance
Lightning Source LLC
LaVergne TN
LVHW041640070526
838199LV00052B/3476